Damen

MOG
the forgetful cat

written and illustrated by

Judith Kerr

Parents' Magazine Press
New York

For our own Mog

First published in the United States of America
by Parents' Magazine Press 1972
ISBN: Trade 0-8193-0544-8, Library 0-8193-0545-6
Library of Congress Catalog Card Number: 75-174598
First published in Great Britain
by William Collins Sons & Co., Ltd., London and Glasgow
Copyright © text and illustrations by Judith Kerr 1970
All rights reserved. Printed in the United States of America

Once there was a cat called Mog and she
lived with a family called Thomas.
Mog was nice but not very clever. She didn't understand
a lot of things. A lot of other things she forgot.
She was a very forgetful cat.

Sometimes she ate her supper.
Then she forgot that
she'd eaten it.

Sometimes she thought
of something in the middle of
washing her leg. Then she forgot
to wash the rest of it.

Once she forgot
that cats can't fly.

But most of all she forgot her cat flap.
The cat flap led from the kitchen
into the garden.
Mog could go out...and in again.
It was her own little door.

The garden always made Mog very excited.
She smelled all the smells.
She chased the birds.
She climbed the trees.
She ran round and round
with a big fluffed-up tail.
And then she forgot the cat flap.
She forgot that she had a cat flap.
She wanted to go back into the house,
but she couldn't remember how.

In the end she sat outside the kitchen window
and meowed until someone let her in.

Afterwards you could always tell where she had sat.
This made Mr. Thomas very sad. He said, "Drat that cat!"
But Debbie said, "She's nice!"

Once Mog had a very bad day.
Even the start of the day was bad.
Mog was still asleep. Then Nicky picked her up.
He hugged her and said, "Nice kitty!"
Mog said nothing.
But she was not very happy.

Then it was breakfast time.
Mog forgot that cats have milk for breakfast.
She forgot that cats only have eggs as a treat.

She ate an egg for her breakfast.
Mrs. Thomas said, "Drat that cat!"
Debbie said, "Nicky doesn't like eggs anyway."

Mog looked through her cat flap. It was raining in the garden.
Mog thought, Perhaps the sun is shining in the street.
When the milkman came she ran out.
The milkman shut the door.

The sun was not shining in the street after all.
It was raining.
A big dog came down the street.
Mog ran.
The dog ran, too.

Mog ran right round the house.
And the dog ran after her.
She climbed over the fence.
She ran through the garden and jumped up
outside the kitchen window.
She meowed a big meow—
very sudden and very loud.

Mrs. Thomas said, "Drat that cat!"
Debbie said, "It wasn't her fault."

Mog was very sleepy.
She found a nice warm, soft place
and went to sleep.
She had a lovely dream.
Mog dreamed that she had wings.

She could fly everywhere.
She could fly faster than the birds,
even quite big birds...
Suddenly she woke up.

Mrs. Thomas said, "Drat that cat!"
Debbie said, "I think you look nicer without a hat."

Debbie gave Mog her supper
and Mog ate it all up.
Then Debbie and Nicky went to bed.

Mog had a rest, too,
but Mr. Thomas wanted to see the fight.
Mr. Thomas said, "Drat that cat!"

Mog thought, Nobody likes me.
Then she thought, Debbie likes me.
Debbie's door was open.
Debbie's bed was warm.
Debbie's hair was soft, like kitten fur.
Mog forgot that Debbie was not a kitten.

Debbie had a dream. It was a bad dream.
It was a dream about a tiger.

The tiger wanted to eat Debbie.
It was licking her hair.

Debbie shouted. Mog jumped.
Mr. and Mrs. Thomas said,
"Drat, drat, DRAT that cat!"
Debbie said nothing.
She was still crying because of the bad dream.

Mog ran out of the room
and right through the house
and out of her cat flap.
She was very sad.
The garden was dark.
The house was dark, too.
Mog sat in the dark
and thought dark thoughts.
She thought: Nobody likes me.
They've all gone to bed.
There's no one to let me in.
And they haven't even given me
my supper.

Then she noticed something.
The house was not quite dark.
There was a little light moving about.
She looked through the window
and saw a man in the kitchen.
Mog thought, Perhaps that man will let me in.
Perhaps he will give me my supper.

She meowed her biggest meow,
very sudden and very, very loud.
The man was surprised.
He dropped his bag.
It made a big noise
and everyone in the house woke up.

Mr. Thomas ran down to the kitchen
and shouted, "A burglar!"
The burglar said, "Drat that cat!"
Mrs. Thomas telephoned the police.
Debbie let Mog in
and Nicky hugged her.

A policeman came and they told him
what had happened. The policeman looked at Mog.
He said, "What a remarkable cat.

"I've seen watch-dogs, but never a watch-cat.
She will get a medal."
Debbie said, "I think she'd rather have an egg."

Mog had a medal.
She also had an egg every day for breakfast.
Mr. and Mrs. Thomas told all their friends about her.
They said, "Mog is really remarkable."
And they never—or almost never—
said, "Drat that cat!"